THE LOST HOUR

A Grand Globetrotting Adventure with Six O'Clock & Friends

By

NICOLA PEARSON

Illustrated by

MAYA KEEGAN

Layout & Graphic Design by Jon-Paul Verfaillie

For my niece, Jessica,
whose curiosity inspired this story.

~N.P.~

Lovingly dedicated to all
of my wonderful grandparents.

~M.K.~

One chilly Sunday in March, in the mountains of Washington State, Stephen got up early and put the hands on his grandfather clock forward an hour, from six o'clock to seven o'clock.

"HEY!" shouted Six O'Clock angrily.
"Hey! Whoa! What about me? Hey, I was ready for work, honest. I brushed my teeth and everything...

YOU CAN'T JUST

DING!

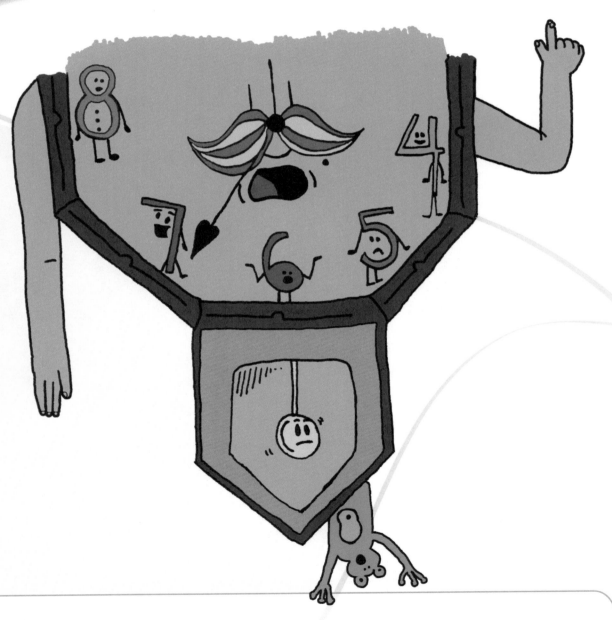

"Sorry," said Grandfather Clock,
"but it strikes me that you are now unemployed."

"What?" exclaimed Six O'Clock. "But why?"

"Because of daylight-savings time,"
explained Grandfather Clock. "The people lose
an hour so the days will stay lighter later."

"But that's not fair!" complained Six O'Clock. "Why would they want to lose me? I've always been on time, I say my chimes correctly..."

"I don't like to be
T O C K I N G
when I'm supposed to be
T I C K I N G ."

"You'd better just pack your bags and be on your way, lad," said Grandfather Clock kindly.

Six O'Clock bravely wiped away a tear, and stepped out of the grandfather clock.

"Goodbye, hours," he called sadly.

"GOODBYE!" they chimed. "AND GOOD LUCK!"

"I'll miss you," whispered Five O'Clock.

"Good old Five O'Clock!" thought Six O'Clock to himself. They'd had some fun changing hands together.

Six O'Clock decided to go east to look for a job. He knew that he could fly (because he had heard people talking about how time flies) so he let himself drift up into the air.

 Pretty soon he was FLYING... flying towards the East Coast!

Six O'Clock landed in New York City and was amazed at how fast everybody moved there. People were always looking at their own little clocks, wishing there were more hours in the day.

"This is great!" thought Six O'Clock. "Maybe I can get a job as an extra hour in the day! That's what these people seem to need."

"GEDOUDDAHIR, KID!" they yelled rudely. "You can't have more than 24 hours in a clock! Besides, we don't need no West Coast time in OUR clocks. People have gotta move FAST in this here city!"

Six O'Clock hung his head in shame. What was he to do? Then he heard music, *beautiful* music. It was coming from the New York City Orchestra.

He flew to the concert hall and found the musicians playing a symphony in 6/4 time. And there were chimes in the percussion!

"This is perfect," he told himself happily. "I can chime in 6/4 time with the best of them."

So, Six O'Clock auditioned for the orchestra, and got the job.

Everything was fine, for a while.
Six O'Clock was very proud of his new position.

"Who needs clocks?" he thought to himself.
"My life is in music. I can see that now"

But just as he was getting settled, the music changed,
to a symphony in 4/4 time. And with a wave of
the conductor's baton, Six O'Clock's career
in the orchestra came to an end.

Once again, Six O'Clock packed
his bags and flew east.
This time, he landed in
another country: 𝕰𝖓𝖌𝖑𝖆𝖓𝖉.

There, he was adopted by a little girl called Elizabeth,
who put him in her mathematics notebook.

Six O'Clock felt very comfortable
in the notebook until, one day,
Elizabeth started doing strange things with him.

She used a two to divide him into two threes...

She took four
away from him,
and left him as
only two...

... Then, **HORROR** of **HORRORS**, she added seven to him, his least favorite number, and turned Six into thirteen!

This was a number Six O'Clock had never heard of before, and he decided that this was too much. It was time to pack his bags and fly further east.

For the next few months, Six O'Clock
went through some *very* tough jobs.

In one country, he found himself on a
vegetable stand, as a price tag for some cabbage.

In another, _____ he was put on the front of a bus.

Then he got a job on a stopwatch, as the six part of sixty seconds. This was more in his line of work, but he did find it tiring to have to dash around the face of the watch in only sixty seconds.

While Six O'Clock was traveling, the spring turned to summer, and the summer turned to fall.

The leaves on the trees were changing color and the days were getting shorter.

One Sunday in November, Six O'Clock realized he was very close to Washington State, where he had lived in the grandfather clock with the other hours. He decided to pay them a visit.

When he arrived, he found Stephen
moving the hands on the clock *back* one hour,
from seven o'clock to six o'clock!

This is the other end of daylight savings time,
when people gain an hour so that
there is light earlier in the morning.

"Oh dear!" groaned Grandfather Clock. "We need an extra six o'clock, because we've gained an hour."

"I can do it! I can do it!" yelled Six O'Clock excitedly. He had arrived just in the nick of time.

"Come on then!" urged Grandfather Clock. "Get up here quickly... You're about to CHIME!"

With that, Six O'Clock climbed back into the grandfather clock and proudly chimed his six chimes. For he was truly happy that he was no longer the hour lost,

but the hour *gained*.

36809935R00022